MIKE TILLES

The Dove Who Learned How to Love

ILLUSTRATED BY SIMON THOMPSON

First published in 2020 by The Roma Group,
The Old National School, 62 North Street,
Bourne, Leicestershire, PE10 9AJ.

This edition published in 2020.

Text © 2020 Mike Tilles
Illustrations © 2020 Simon Thompson

All right reserved. No part of this publication may be reproduced, distributed or transmitted in any form or by any means, including photocopying, recording, or other electronic or mechanical methods, without the prior written permission of the publisher, except in the case of brief quotations embodied in critical reviews and certain other non-commercial uses permitted by copywrite law.

The rights of Mike Tilles and Simon Thompson to be identified as author and illustrator respectively of the work has been asserted by them in accordance with the Copyright, Designs and Patent Act 1988.

Printed in the United Kingdom.

"For Ruth, Ivor and Jemima"

Deep in the forest, high in a tree,
Lived a dove called Geoff who was grumpy as can be.

He'd always tell the children to keep the noise down,
"Just leave me alone!" he'd say with a frown.

He never gave out sweets on Halloween,
He'd just close his curtains looking sullen and mean.

He'd been this way since anyone could remember,
Seven days a week, from January to December.

Meanwhile nearby his brother had been blessed,
With a beautiful baby to add to his nest.

He and his wife were so in love with their girl,
They thought long and hard and named her Pearl.

Her mum taught her how to find food and water,
Her father told the world of his wonderful daughter.

But Uncle Geoff never visited which they thought was a shame,
They tried and tried but he just never came.

One day while admiring their perfect baby dove,
They suddenly heard some shouts from above.

"Fly away!" came the cry "Everybody must go!"
"You must try to hide because I spy a crow!"

The parents said "Pearl, we are under attack!"
"You need to stay still and hide under this sack."

"We'll come back as soon as we've escaped from the crow,"
"But in the meantime look out for anyone you know."

The next morning Geoff went out to post a letter,
He was angry and frowning and grumpy as ever.

He dropped the letter into the box with his beak,
When all of a sudden he heard someone speak.

"Uncle Geoff" said the voice. "I'm under this sack."
"My parents hid me here but they haven't come back."

"Stay there then" snapped Geoff "I'm not in the mood!"
"But I'm hungry" said Pearl "And I could do with some food."

"Fine then" said Geoff. "You can come to my nest."
"It's a little bit messy; you're my first ever guest."

After their lunch Pearl said, "Can we play?
Or maybe draw a picture? Or do some ballet?"

"Fine" spluttered Geoff, trying not to sound sour.
"My crossword puzzle can wait for an hour."

So they played and laughed and by the next day,
Geoff's outlook was sunnier and a little less grey.

She taught him to sing and tie plaits in her hair,
And how to race cars and dress up her bear.

And how to play tag and how to do yoga,
And how to make a fort just using a sofa.

And suddenly Geoff felt he was starting to change,
He smiled all the time which was ever so strange.

Meanwhile her parents had escaped from the crow
And returned to the sack but Pearl wasn't below.

They looked high and low, they searched every tree,
When finally they said "I know where she'll be."

"Pearl, is that you?" said her mum with a grin.
"We've missed you so much… I don't know where to begin!"

So Pearl explained how she'd waited under the sack,
For nearly a day but they hadn't come back.

And how Geoff had helped her – he'd been ever so kind.
And how she'd had the most wonderful time.

"Ok then" said Geoff, "I guess this is goodbye"
Trying hard to conceal the tear in his eye.

"Thank you" said the parents "We don't know what to say."
"We'll make sure she comes back to visit each day."

So from then on each morning Pearl came to his nest,
And Geoff always smiled and never seemed stressed.

And it goes to show, no matter how old the dove,
It's never too late to learn how to love.

About the Author

Mike grew up in Wimbledon, south-west London and, after gaining a degree in French and Sports Coaching from Oxford Brookes University, enjoyed 12 years working as a French and Spanish teacher in outer London and Surrey.

Mike's passion for poetry started at a young age with his mother still possessing several poems dating back to his primary school days. Having written poems for his wife Ruth over the course of a number of years (including his marriage proposal), he decided to use the extra time afforded to him during the Covid-19 related lockdown of 2020 to fulfil the lifelong ambition of turning this interest into the creation of a series of children's books. Along with *The Dove Who Learned How to Love*, he has also written *The Shark who was Scared of the Dark* and *The King who Couldn't Sing*.

As well as being a keen amateur sportsman, Mike has a passion for music and takes inspiration from the clever lyrics and wordplay of the likes of Bob Dylan and the Arctic Monkeys.

Mike lives in Twickenham with Ruth and their two children, Ivor and Jemima.

About the Illustrator

Simon started designing book covers straight after finishing Art School, before establishing his career designing and illustrating books and magazines.
After having a stroke in 2018 he now specialises in contemporary portraits and limited edition commissions while continuing with his passion of illustration.

He loves film, Bisley and Disco.

Simon lives in North London, has two girls, Rose and Hannah and Walnut the cat.